DATE DUE

GAYLORD			PRINTED IN U.S.A.

COUNTING SHEEP

Counting Sheep

By John Archambault
Illustrated by John Rombola

Henry Holt and Company · New York

I'm all tucked in bed.
I can't go to sleep.
I'm still wide awake.
I'm tired of counting sheep.

I need to count
with a little pizzazz . . .

One rhino-rhinoceros!
Now that's razzmatazz!

Two tall giraffes
are my ladder to the moon,

where I play hide-and-seek
with three raccoons.

Now I slide to the stars
on four dinosaurs.

Flip-a-tail, one swoosh!
Two! Three! Four!

Five wide-eyed owls
ride the Ferris wheel.

Six cats spin cotton candy
for a midnight meal.

Eight lazy alligators
serenade the moon.

Nine ponytailed ponies
come to carry me home.

Giddy up! Giddy up!
I ride the night alone . . .

flying through the sky . . .
the night is dark and deep . . .
I'm a falling star . . .
falling . . .
1
2
3
4

slowly
softly
falling more

5
6
gently down

7
8
homeward bound

slowly
      softly
silently . . .
    9

10
stars in my pocket . . .
all mine to keep . . .

falling . . .
    dreamily . . .
        streamily . . .

fast asleep. . . .

To Crystal Jean Neill,
whom I count among the stars in my pocket

Text copyright © 1989 by John Archambault
Illustrations copyright © 1989 by John Rombola

Published by Henry Holt and Company, Inc.,
115 West 18th Street, New York, New York 10011.
Published in Canada by Fitzhenry & Whiteside Limited,
195 Allstate Parkway, Markham, Ontario L3R 4T8.
This book has previously been published in
different formats by DLM Teaching Resources.

Library of Congress Cataloging-in-Publication Data
Archambault, John.
    Counting sheep / by John Archambault ; illustrated by John
    Rombola.
    Summary: Tired of counting sheep, a child counts other imaginative
animals to fall asleep.
    ISBN 0-8050-1135-8
    (1. Stories in rhyme.   2. Counting—Fiction.   3. Sleep—Fiction.)
I. Rombola, John, ill.   II. Title.
PZ8.3.A584Co   1989
(E)—dc20   89-11163

Henry Holt books are available at special discounts
for bulk purchases for sales promotions, premiums,
fund-raising, or educational use. Special editions
or book excerpts can also be created to specification.

    For details contact:

    Special Sales Director
    Henry Holt and Company, Inc.
    115 West 18th Street
    New York, New York, 10011

First Edition
Printed in Hong Kong
10 9 8 7 6 5 4 3 2 1